MW01137226

Once Upon A Small Town

By John Mooy

Illustrated by Wendy Anderson Halperin

EDCO Publishing, Inc.

EDCO Publishing, Inc.
2648 Lapeer Road
Auburn Hills, MI 48326
1-888-510-3326
www.edcopublishing.com

First Edition: March 2010

ISBN-13   978-0-9798088-3-8

Library of Congress Control Number: 2010922784

10 9 8 7 6 5 4 3 2

Printed in the United States of America.

For Mae and the people of Marcellus

If you are from, or live in Marcellus,
then you know, 49067.
You are also a "Wildcat." You read the only newspaper in the
world that cares about your town, and you have a favorite story
about Jimmy Shannon, known to the "locals" simply as -
Jimmy.

Many, many years have passed since Jimmy's Mom,
said to him, "I am going to take you home and teach
you to do nice things." She spent her life showing
Jimmy exactly what she meant.

Jimmy understood her lessons well and
today he is teaching us.

"Thank you, Mae, and Go 'Cellus!"

JM

Dedicated To:
John and his small town, Edna and her big ideas,
my mom who never gave up on getting this story told, and
Jimmy.

WAH

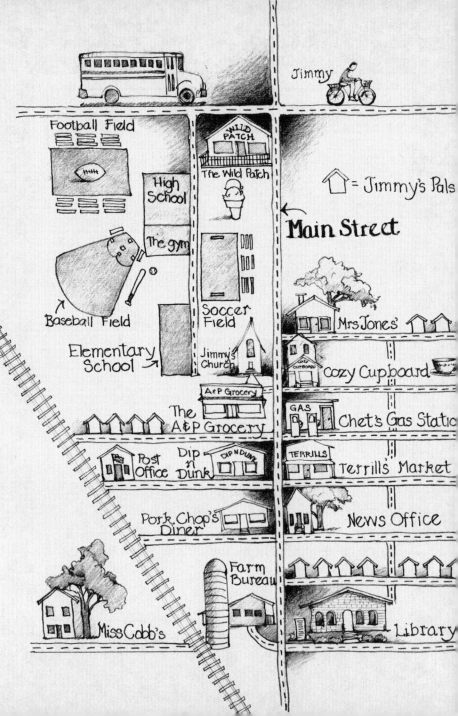

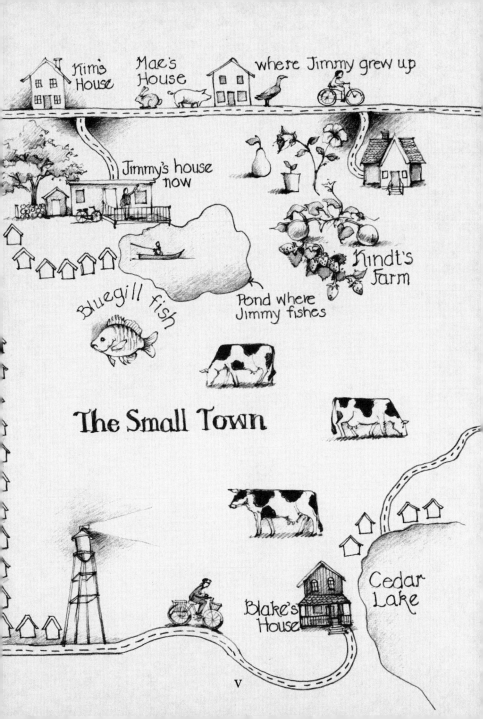

Kim's House

Mae's House

where Jimmy grew up

Jimmy's house now

Kindt's Farm

Bluegill fish

Pond where Jimmy fishes

The Small Town

Blake's House

Cedar Lake

Chapters

A Small Town Story Begins

At night, I could watch the revolving light on top of the water tower as it made circles in the sky. After a road trip in the backseat of my parents' car, it was comforting to look out the window and see that light, which meant we were almost home. Home was Marcellus, a small town of eleven hundred people in southwest Michigan.

One night as we were driving home, I heard my parents talking about how Marcellus and other small towns across America were disappearing. That made me feel sad. But then Mom and Dad went on to say the memories of these small towns would never disappear as long as there were people to share their stories. That's when I decided to share the best story I know about our little town, so others can continue to pass it along.

It all began at Marcellus School one Monday morning just after lunch count. Mrs. Elsey, my fifth grade teacher, got up from her desk and walked to the chalkboard in the front of the classroom. Mrs. Elsey can write on the board in a straight line and never makes the chalk screech. All eyes were on her as she picked up the chalk. Without saying a word, she began to write. Everyone read along as she wrote:

YOUR ASSIGNMENT:

1. You will be a **news reporter** (like Mr. Moormann at the **Marcellus News** office).

2. You will look for an interesting story about our small town.

3. Your story can be about a **person**, **place** or **thing** (your choice).

4. Once you have chosen a topic, make a list of what you want to find out and what you think might be interesting to others. (Your mom and dad may help you with this part of the assignment.)

6. You will **interview** people to find out information about your topic. (Be sure to use your best manners as you interview each person.)

7. You will write notes and other information in your interview notebook.

Then Mrs. Elsey stopped writing, turned and faced the class and said, "Because this is such a big assignment you will have several weeks to finish it. This will be fun because you can choose a topic that interests you or one that you are curious about."

Mrs. Elsey placed the big box that had been sitting by the door onto her desk. She told us she had purchased an interview notebook for each of us from **Ingersoll's Drugstore**. She had printed a name on the front of each notebook in black letters. When she read my name, I walked up to her desk and got my notebook. As I walked back to my seat I thought about the assignment on the board. I didn't think I wanted to report on a **place** or **thing**. Places and things usually just sit somewhere and don't move around a whole lot. Reporting about a place or thing didn't sound like much fun to me! I'll ask Mom and Dad about some ideas at dinner tonight, I thought.

At the end of the day, I headed out the door of the school with my new interview notebook tucked under my arm and one important question in my head: **What is interesting, found in Marcellus, and moves a lot?**

The Great Idea

At dinner that evening, I sat in my usual place at the kitchen table. My sister sat across from me and my mom and dad sat across from each other, as they always did.

"How was school today, Kenna?" Dad asked.

"Fine," she replied between mouthfuls of mac and cheese.

"And Blake, how was school for you today?" Mom asked. These were the same questions they asked us every night at the supper table.

"Good," I answered, "Mrs. Elsey gave us a big assignment and she said we could ask our parents for help."

"What's the big assignment?" asked Kenna with a puzzled look on her face along with some cheese.

I smiled at my sister and continued, "Mrs. Elsey wrote the assignment on the board and told us we would be reporters like Mr. Moormann at the **News** office. That we could choose to write about a person, place or thing in Marcellus. We have to find interesting information about our topic by interviewing people and then write it in the interview notebook she gave us."

"She gave you a notebook, Blake?" asked Kenna.

"She did, and it has my name in big letters on the front," I replied, as I looked at my sister and grinned while she wiped the cheese off her face onto her napkin.

"I really don't want to write about a place or thing," I said. "I want to write about something that's more active, something that moves. So I guess I would have to write about a person, but I'm just not sure who that would be."

As soon as I had finished my sentence, Kenna got up from the table and headed to the refrigerator for more milk. She stopped at the window and began tapping and waving.

"What are you doing, Kenna?" asked dad.

"I'm waving," she said.

"At who?" he asked.

"At Jimmy," she said. "He's on his bike"

"It must be Jimmy Shannon," I said.

"It is," said Kenna, sitting back down with her glass of milk.

Dad looked quizzically across the table at me with a raised eyebrow and asked, "Blake, do you know anybody in this town who is on the move more than Jimmy Shannon?"

"No, I don't, Dad. Jimmy is everywhere. He rides his bike, he walks and he runs," I said as I looked back at him with my 'I get it' look.

"Thanks, Dad, I'll write about Jimmy". Everyone in town knows Jimmy, and he's always going somewhere and doing something."

The Story "Leads"

For the next week, I asked everyone I saw about Jimmy Shannon. I talked to both Mr. Thornton, who helped out at the **News** office, and to Mr. Moormann, who ran the **News** office. I talked to Clara at the **Cozy Cupboard Restaurant**, where Jimmy sometimes stopped for snacks. I talked to Mrs. Gooding whose house Jimmy rode by almost every day and where he often stopped to visit with her. Everyone had something to say about Jimmy, and most of them suggested another person I should interview.

"You should talk to Mr. Townsend at the post office," said Mr. Thornton. His three sons used to play ball with Jimmy after he finished baling hay on their farm.

Mrs. Lynn at the grocery story told me I should talk to Mr. Kindt because Jimmy had worked for him.

Mr. Pantale at the **Dip and Dunk Restaurant** told me I should talk to Mrs. Jones. "She was a friend of Jimmy's mother, Mae, and thought the world of her," he said.

Mr. Terrill at the meat market said, "You should talk to your Grandpa Jack because he and Jimmy both like sports, and they are in the same Lions Club together. Mr. Porath is in the Lions Club too."

One morning before school, I told Mrs. Elsey I had chosen Jimmy Shannon as the topic for my assignment. "Blake, that's a great idea. Jimmy certainly is a fellow on the move, and he has been an important part of our town for a long time now. Good luck on your story," she said with a reassuring smile.

I knew I had chosen a good topic for my assignment.

The List

I spent the next week gathering names of people around Marcellus that I could talk to, and ideas for stories I could talk to them about. I was excited to get started on the assignment about Jimmy Shannon, "the Marcellus man in motion."

Each evening, I sat at the kitchen table with my notebook. With help from Mom and Dad, I came up with a list of ideas for my story:

- Jimmy in his early years
- Jimmy and Mae
- Jimmy and his bike
- Jimmy finally talks
- Jimmy at Kindt's farm
- Jimmy and Clara at the **Cozy Cupboard**
- Jimmy and Mrs. Gooding
- Jimmy, the teams, and at the games
- Jimmy in the **Lions Club**
- Jimmy's school degree
- Jimmy's own home

Blake's Story Begins

After school, I jumped on my shiny red bike with the interview notebook tucked in the front of my shirt and my pencil in my pocket. I pedaled down the street to see Mrs. Jones. Mrs. Jones lived alone in a brick house near the edge of town. I rolled into the driveway, parked my bike, walked up to the front door, rang the doorbell and waited.

Mrs. Jones opened the door and smiled.

"Come in, Blake. What are you up to today?" she asked, in her pleasant soft-spoken voice.

"I have an assignment for school. I'm writing a story about Jimmy Shannon and I thought you could help me with some of the details," I told her.

"Jimmy is one of my favorite people, I'd be happy to help," she replied with a grin. "What would you like to know?" As I pulled out my notebook and pencil I told her all about the assignment.

"Have a seat," she said, pointing to the couch as she sat down in a big comfortable-looking chair across from me.

"Mrs. Jones, do you remember when Jimmy was born?" I asked. "I really don't know much about Jimmy's birth," she replied.

"Do you know where Jimmy was born?" I asked.

"You know, Blake, I don't know that anyone in town knows exactly where Jimmy was born," Mrs. Jones said thoughtfully.

"I was born in Kalamazoo," I told her with a puzzled look on my face. "I thought everybody knew where they were born."

"Most people do know where they were born, but Jimmy's story is a little different," she said.

"How is it different?" I asked.

"Mae Shannon was a good friend of mine and had always wanted a child. She and her husband adopted Jimmy when he was two years old. Mae became Jimmy's mom and brought him to live here in Marcellus." I wrote in my notebook as fast as I could as Mrs. Jones continued her story.

"Mae's husband died at an early age, so she had to raise Jimmy all by herself. Mae was one of the most wonderful people who ever lived in Marcellus. She loved Jimmy very much. She taught him to do so many nice things and to treat people with kindness."

Mrs. Jones paused, looked at me with a smile and said, "Blake, I just took some chocolate chip cookies out of the oven. Would you like some?" Without waiting for my answer, she got up from her chair and headed toward the kitchen.

"Yes, Ma'am, that would be great," I told her as I continued writing notes in my notebook.

She soon returned from the kitchen with a plate of cookies and put it on the table next to me. I took one bite of cookie and said, "Umm, these are really good. Mrs. Jones, can you tell me anything else about Mae and Jimmy?"

Mrs. Jones sighed and continued, "Blake, when Jimmy was a little boy, maybe seven or eight years old, the doctors told Mae she should put him in a home for the developmentally challenged."

"Mae didn't want to do it, but because she thought it would be good for Jimmy, she followed the doctor's advice. She took Jimmy to a facility in a nearby town where she had to leave him."

"Overnight?" I asked. "All by himself?"

"Well, it was going to be for much longer than just overnight," Mrs. Jones continued. "The Doctor said Jimmy would most likely have to stay there all his life."

"Then how did Jimmy get back to Marcellus, Mrs. Jones?" I asked.

"Well, I'm glad to tell you that this is where Jimmy's story begins to get somewhat happier," she said with a smile.

"Mae went to visit Jimmy at the home every day. And every day she would find him sitting in a chair in the corner of a room staring at the floor. But Mae didn't give up, Blake, she continued to visit Jimmy every single day, hoping he would improve," said Mrs. Jones.

"Then what happened?" I asked anxiously, sitting up on the edge of the couch.

"Then one day after Jimmy had been there a few weeks, Mae decided to bring him home. The story goes that Mae said to him, 'Jimmy, I love you and I'm going to take you home and teach you to do nice things.' That was the day she brought Jimmy home, for good," Mrs. Jones said, with tears in her eyes.

For a moment or two, we both just sat there quietly looking at each other. Then I stood up and said, "I'd better get going, Mrs. Jones." I took one more cookie from the plate for the ride home.

I tucked my notebook into the front of my shirt and put my pencil in my pocket. Mrs. Jones walked me to the door and opened it. "Thank you. You have given me a lot of information," I said.

"You're very welcome," she said. "I'd like to read your story when it's finished."

"Sure," I said, as I pulled my leg up over the seat of my bike and put my foot down on the pedal. I stood for a moment and then turned, and looked back at her.

"Mrs. Jones, I'm glad Mae brought Jimmy back home from that place," I said.

"We all are, Blake" she replied, waving to me as I rode out of the driveway.

I waved back and shouted, "Thanks for the cookies!"

Jimmy on the Move

In the following days, I discovered if I carried my interview notebook with me, people would often ask me what I was writing. I would not only tell them, but also show them what I had written so far about Jimmy Shannon. Everybody I talked to knew something about Jimmy and had a favorite story to tell.

One sunny day after school as I was walking down Main Street, I ran into Mr. Thornton. Mr. Thornton was a sixth grade teacher and worked at the **News** office in his spare time. He liked history and had written many interesting stories for the newspaper.

"Hi, Blake, I see you have your notebook with you. Are you writing a big story?" he asked with a smile.

"Kind of, Mr. Thornton. It's for an assignment Mrs. Elsey gave us. I'm writing about Jimmy Shannon," opening my notebook up to show him.

"Could I ask you about Jimmy, Mr. Thornton?"

"Of course, how can I help you?"

"Do you remember what Jimmy was like when he was little?" I asked.

"Of course I do, Blake. Let's sit down and I'll tell you."

I sat down next to Mr. Thornton on the lone step that led up to the landing of Ingersoll's Drugstore.

"When Jimmy was younger, maybe ten or eleven, I remember he used

to help his mom on the farm. They would take care of the animals and worked together to grow flowers and other things. Jimmy really liked the farm. Even when he was little, it seemed he was always busy and on the go. He and his mom raised chickens and ducks. Jimmy was very gentle with the animals and followed them around.

He and Mae would ride into town almost every day. Some days they would go to the **Farm Bureau** to buy bags of feed for the chickens and ducks. Even though Jimmy was little, he was very strong. He would lift those heavy bags and put them in the trunk of the car," said Mr. Thornton, going through the motion of lifting a bag of feed as he spoke. "Then Jimmy and Mae would make several stops right here on Main Street. They'd go into the **A&P®** store for groceries, into the **News** office on Thursdays to get the paper, and back to **Chet's City Service** gas station to put gas in their car. The gas station was once right there across the street," said Mr. Thornton, pointing to the lot where the station used to be. "There was a big stone fountain on that corner. You had to go up two steps and lean over to get a drink of water. Jimmy liked to get a drink there while Big Chet filled their car with gasoline."

"Did you get all that written down, Blake?" Mr. Thornton asked with a chuckle, knowing that it would have been almost impossible for me to write down everything he had said.

"Not all of it, but Mrs. Elsey said we could just write some notes to help us remember the story and later we could write the details," I said, looking up at Mr. Thornton with a grin.

"And Mrs. Elsey is absolutely right. That's what good reporters do," Mr. Thornton told me with a big grin.

"So you could say, Blake, that Jimmy didn't let any grass grow under his feet."

"What's that mean?" I asked.

"It means, that Jimmy was always on the move. He was never still."

"Another interesting thing about Jimmy," Mr. Thorton continued, "when he was young, and went to all those places with his mom, everyone would always say, 'Hi, Jimmy,' or 'Hi, Jimmy, how are you today?' or 'I see you're helping your mom today, Jimmy,' or 'Must be those chickens and ducks have to eat today.' Everywhere Jimmy went, everyone would take time to talk to him."

"And what did Jimmy say, Mr. Thornton?"

"He didn't say anything, Blake, he just looked at them."

"He didn't talk?" I asked, looking very surprised.

"No, Jimmy didn't speak until he was all grown up, but he always looked at people like he understood what they were saying."

"I have to find out more about that, Mr. Thornton, because Jimmy sure talks now," I told him.

"One more thing, Blake. When Jimmy got to be a little older, he started riding his bike into town almost every day. When he got into town, he would go to the same places he and his mom went together."

"And did people still talk to Jimmy, Mr. Thornton?"

"Yes they did, Blake."

"And did Jimmy say anything?" I asked.

"No, but he sure liked to be near those people he knew, and they looked forward to having Jimmy just stop by to visit for awhile. He was on that bike all the time, either coming to town or going home. Jimmy has probably ridden a million miles by now."

"Blake, would you like to go into the drugstore and have a pop or an ice cream cone?" asked Mr. Thornton.

"Thank you, but I'd better be getting home. And, besides, my mom always says, if I eat something at this time of day I won't be hungry for supper," I said with a grin.

"She's probably right," he replied with a chuckle. "Okay, keep up the good work on your story. I'd love to read it when you're finished."

"Sure, Mr. Thornton, and thanks for your help." I told him as I started down the street. I hadn't gone far when I whirled around and said, "Mr. Thornton, who would know when Jimmy first began to talk?"

"Why don't you ask Mr. Townsend at the post office. He might know, because he knows just about everyone in town," said Mr. Thornton.

"Thanks," I said, as I waved and walked toward home.

A Good Thought

That evening, as I sat at the kitchen table ready to eat supper,
I thought about what Mrs. Jones had told me that afternoon. I looked
at my family seated around the table, as they were every evening.
I thought about Jimmy's life when he was my age and how different it
must have been from mine.

Another Day At School

Sitting at her desk at the front of the room, Mrs. Elsey told us, "The word on the street is that students from our class have been interviewing people around town and gathering information for their stories. Sounds like all of you are becoming real reporters."

I opened my notebook to take a quick look at my notes before class began. I glanced down at "Jimmy's First Words," written at the top of the blank page. I wondered when he first spoke, and what he said? After school today, I will try to find the answers to those questions, I vowed. I closed my notebook and got ready for the weekly spelling test. Writing about Jimmy Shannon was fun. Mrs. Elsey was right again.

The Day Jimmy Talked

After school, I followed the sidewalk on the north side of the school. I cut diagonally across the playground ending at the street next to the railroad tracks. From there, it was a very short walk across the tracks to the post office.

I walked past the tall glass panels and through the door with the metal numbers, **49067,** the zip code for Marcellus, hanging above it.

"Hi, Mr. Townsend," I said, as I walked into the lobby and up to the counter.

"Hi, Blake," he said with a smile. "What brings you into the post office today?"

"I'll show you," I said, placing my notebook on the counter. "I'm writing a story about Jimmy Shannon for Mrs. Elsey's class," I told him as I flipped through the pages of my notebook, so he could see what I had written so far.

"Mr. Thornton told me I should talk to you about the next part of the story."

"What's the next part of your story?" he asked.

"I'm trying to find out when Jimmy first started to talk," I said, pulling the pencil out of my pocket. "Did you know Jimmy when he didn't talk?" I asked.

"Yes, I did," he replied.

"Have you known Jimmy for a long time?" I continued as I began to take notes.

"I sure have. Why, I knew Jimmy long before you were even born," Mr. Townsend told me with a grin.

"Do you have any idea who might know about the first time Jimmy spoke?" I asked, ready to write his reply.

"Yes I do," said Mr. Townsend, running his hand through his hair.

"Do I know them?" I asked.

"Yes you do, Blake," he said with a smile.

"Good! Where can I find them?" I asked.

"Right here, Blake," said Mr. Townsend, now with an even bigger smile. "I was there when Jimmy said his first word."

"Will you tell me about it?"

"I'd be happy to Blake, but first, let me give this lady her mail," he said, handing several letters across the counter to Mrs. Richardson who had just walked in. She put them into her purse with a quick wave as Mr. Townsend went on, "Okay, it was quite a while ago now but here's what I remember. In the summertime Jimmy used to help farmers when they baled hay. He would often ride on top of a big wagonload of hay being delivered to my farm," said Mr. Townsend.

"One hot summer day, Jimmy had helped stack hay in the barn. My three boys and some of the neighbor kids were playing ball in our

backyard. When Jimmy finished his work he stood at the edge of the ball field and watched the boys play and have fun. One of them asked him if he would like to play with them. Of course, Jimmy didn't say anything, but the boys included him in the game and showed him what to do. They all had a great time. When the game was finished, everyone was hot and sweaty. My wife came out of the house and asked, 'Who's thirsty?'"

"Everyone yelled, 'I am! I am!' and then told her what they wanted to drink," Mr. Townsend went on. "Everyone, except Jimmy. My wife walked over and stood by Jimmy and asked, 'Jimmy, what would you like to drink?' Jimmy looked up at her, smiled and said, 'POP!'"

"Wow, then what happened?" I asked, excited to know more.

"All of us just stood there and stared at Jimmy. We couldn't believe we had just heard him speak for the first time," said Mr. Townsend.

"We looked at each other and then all of us cheered."

"That's amazing," I told him.

"I agree," said Mr. Townsend, "and the most amazing part is that Jimmy was twenty-five years old when he spoke his first word, 'pop'."

"Thanks, Mr. Townsend," I said and headed out the door with my notebook, pencil, and a big smile on my face.

"You're welcome, Blake. Jimmy is really something" he said as he turned around and began putting mail into the postal boxes.

More At the Table

That evening at the supper table, just like every evening since I had started the assignment about Jimmy Shannon, my sister, mom and dad wanted to know how the story was progressing. Each day, I told them I had found another story and there were more questions to be answered about Jimmy.

As I finished a piece of mom's yummy apple pie, I looked at her and asked, "How long have you and Dad known Jimmy?"

"Jimmy has been in Marcellus my entire life," she told me, "I can remember when I would go places in the car with your grandma and grandpa, we would always see Jimmy riding his bike along the road."

"Jimmy's been riding a bike as long as I can remember," said dad.

"Wow, that's a lot of bike riding. Has he always had the same bike?" asked Kenna.

I picked up my notebook, which I now kept with me all the time.

"Actually," dad said, "Jimmy wears out a bike every couple of years. He rides it in the rain, the snow, and on hot summer days. Jimmy rides his bike year round. Why, I remember once during Christmas season, he even had a small Christmas tree tied on the back fender of his bike." Everybody at the table smiled, picturing a Christmas tree strapped to the back of Jimmy's bike as he rode down the street.

"Where does Jimmy get a new bike?" I asked with my notebook open and pencil in hand.

"When Jimmy's bike is finally worn out, a note appears in bold letters on the front window of the **Marcellus News**," said Dad.

"A note?" asked Kenna. "What does it say?"

"It just says, "JIMMY NEEDS A NEW BIKE", replied Dad.

"And then what happens?" Kenna asked.

"People in Marcellus stop by the **News** office and leave money to pay for Jimmy's new bike. When there's enough money, someone takes Jimmy to the bicycle shop in Kalamazoo. He gets to choose a new bike in the color he likes. Jimmy loves that!" Dad told us with a smile.

"Jimmy's legs just keep on going," said Kenna. "Besides riding his bike, I've also seen him walking and running. Jimmy is really something."

"He's always on the move," I replied.

"Yes," Mom added, "On summer evenings, I've seen Jimmy riding his bike home along the road so many times he seemed to be part of the sunset."

Some Interesting Facts

It was Friday, Mrs. Elsey often made her tasty, homemade, chocolate and peanut butter fudge for the class if they did their best on the weekly spelling test. Today, she had brought five plates filled with her sweet delicious fudge.

After the test, Mrs. Elsey asked the person sitting at the front of each row to come to the front of the class. She handed each of them a plate of fudge. They gave each person in their row two pieces of the special treat.

"Class, while you're eating your fudge, I want you to check the notes in your notebook. Think about your story and who you will interview next for interesting facts and details," said Mrs. Elsey. "To be a good reporter, you should work steadily on your story. Write some each day and do not leave a lot to do at the last minute," she told us.

"Has anyone found something interesting in their interviews they would like to share?" she asked. Doug raised his hand.

"Douglas, what have you found out?" she asked.

"I'm researching some of the buildings in Marcellus. I found out there used to be a two-story outhouse just behind Main Street, not far from where John Decker's barbershop once was," said Doug. Some of the kids laughed out loud.

"That's interesting, Douglas," Mrs. Elsey said with a smile.

Doug went on, "And one time there was a tall, old, brick building next to the railroad tracks that was a popcorn factory. Some people say it is

29

haunted, but I don't know if that's a fact."

"Very nice reporting, Douglas," said Mrs. Elsey. "Does anyone else have something interesting to share?"

Next, Mrs. Elsey called on Patty who was waving her hand in the air.

"I'm not studying buildings, but I'm finding out some interesting things that have happened in certain places in town," said Patty.

"And something very interesting happened in my backyard," she said.

"Right in your own backyard, Patty?" asked Mrs. Elsey. "Please tell us about it."

Everyone in class looked at Patty and listened as she began to tell her story.

"My dad was working the night shift at the factory in Cassopolis. One night, as he pulled his truck into the driveway, the headlights shone across our backyard. My dad couldn't believe what he saw," she paused as everyone listened and waited for her to continue, "Standing right there in our backyard was a very big elephant."

"An elephant!" Mrs. Elsey exclaimed. "Please, Patty, tell us more."

"It was a real elephant," said Patty, "but what we didn't know was that the circus was in town. They had camped on the football field at the end of our street. The elephant had gotten loose and walked down the street and into our yard," she said, with a big smile on her face.

"Boys and girls, I think you are finding there are some very interesting things about our small town," said Mrs. Elsey. "Now all of you have a fun, safe weekend, and I will see you bright and early on Monday morning. Good luck with your interviewing over the weekend."

Once we were out the door, we scattered in all directions. Some kids walked home, some got on the school buses, and others rode their bikes. I ran all three blocks home without stopping once. I was ready to "investigate" the next part of my story, and I wanted to get out to Mr. Kindt's farm.

"Hi Mom," I yelled, as I ran through the doorway into the kitchen. "Will you drive me out to Mr. Kindt's farm?"

"Why do you want to go to Mr. Kindt's?" she asked.

"It's the next part of my story about Jimmy," I said, as I poured myself a glass of milk.

"This is getting to be quite a story," said mom.

"Well, Jimmy is quite a person," I replied as I finished off the milk and put the empty glass in the sink.

"Give me a minute to grab my purse. I'll meet you in the car," she said.

On the drive out to Mr. Kindt's, Mom talked about Jimmy and how many times he had ridden his bike, to town and back, through the years.

She pulled the car into the parking area in front of Mr. Kindt's roadside stand. I jumped out of the car and, as usual, had my notebook and was ready to write as soon as I found Mr. Kindt. "I'll be buying some fruit and vegetables while you interview Mr. Kindt," Mom said.

It was Mr. Kindt who spotted me first, as he looked up from his work at the produce stand.

"Hi, Blake, how are you today?" he asked.

"Oh, I'm good," I said. "Can I please interview you for my school project?"

"As long as it isn't about math," said Mr. Kindt, with a laugh.

"It isn't, it's about Jimmy Shannon. I'm writing a story about him," I explained.

"Jimmy is one of my favorite people," said Mr. Kindt resting his hands in the side pockets of his overalls.

"What do you want to know about Jimmy?" he asked.

"Mrs. Lynn at the grocery store said I should talk to you because Jimmy used to work for you," I said, pulling the pencil out of my pocket.

"He did work for me, Blake. In fact, I think Jimmy has worked for just about everybody you know. He's raked leaves, baled hay, shoveled snow and mowed yards. He's a hard worker. Come sit down and let's talk about my friend, Jimmy." He began. "A few summers back, Jimmy rode his bike over here and said to me, 'Need work.'"

"So I gave Jimmy a patch of ground right over there," said Mr. Kindt, pointing to a spot next to the barn. "That's where Jimmy grew his cantaloupes. He raked the soil, planted the seeds, and watered those plants all summer. At the end of the summer he had grown lots and lots of cantaloupes! Jimmy learned when small ants show up on the stems of the cantaloupes, they were ready to be picked."

"Jimmy would ride his bike here every day. He would stay and work until it was time to quit."

"What time did he quit working?" I asked.

"When school was in session he would see the school buses pass. That's how Jimmy would tell time," said Mr. Kindt, "and that's when he would quit for the day."

I quickly wrote in my notebook. Mr. Kindt said, "Looks like you have a lot of information in there, Blake."

"Well, there's a lot to write about Jimmy," I replied, with a shrug.

"So what happened next, Mr. Kindt?" I asked.

"After Jimmy's cantaloupes started to ripen, I made a sign for him," said Mr. Kindt. The sign said: I CAN NOT READ OR MAKE CHANGE … CANTALOUPES $1.00."

Mr. Kindt went on with the story. "Every day Jimmy would sell all his cantaloupes. People would also give him tips because he helped them carry the cantaloupes and other things to their cars."

"Jimmy turned into a real helper around the farm. We had so much

I can't make change
$1.00 cantelopes

fun that he started working here in the wintertime too."

"What did he do in the winter?" I asked.

"He worked in the greenhouse. That's the glass building where we grow plants in small pots in wintertime," Mr. Kindt continued.

"As the plants grew, Jimmy would put them into bigger pots. He liked working with plants. He also liked the music we played in the greenhouse," said Mr. Kindt. "Sometimes, on nice summer evenings, Jimmy would spend the night here and sleep in a tent," he said. "We always tell people, 'everything on this farm is raised on love and that included Jimmy.'"

"Now, are you ready to hear about one of the most fun things we continue to do here with Jimmy?" asked Mr. Kindt, with a big smile on his face.

"Yes, what is it?" I asked.

"Every year, on August 21, we have a big birthday party. On that day we celebrate Jimmy's birthday and mine, because he and I share the same birthday," said Mr. Kindt.

"People come to the farm from all around. We have presents, cake and punch. We have a great time. One year a picture of our party was on the front page of the **Marcellus News**."

"Each year I give Jimmy his favorite birthday gift," said Mr. Kindt.

"What's that?" I asked.

"The best present you can give Jimmy is your friendship and a hug. Anything else I can tell you, Blake?" asked Mr. Kindt, getting up from the bench.

"I think that's good, Mr. Kindt. Thank you for helping me. I'll see you later," I told him as I put my notebook under my arm and my pencil in my pocket.

As I headed back to the car, Mr. Kindt waved and called out in a loud voice, "I'd like to read your story when it's finished."

"Sure, Mr. Kindt," I said as I waved goodbye. I hope Mom is making an apple pie, I thought as I helped her put the two big bags of apples and a bag of vegetables into the car. Then, we headed for home and guess who we saw riding his bike from town?

At the "Cozy"

It was autumn, a beautiful time of the year in Marcellus. The leaves were changing color, and the sky was a beautiful blue. The days were sunny and the nights were getting cooler.

On this beautiful fall day as I rode my bike down Main Street, I noticed the bench in front of the **Cozy Cupboard** Restaurant. I knew the bench had been put there for Jimmy. He would sit on the bench, and wave to people as they passed by in their cars, trucks, and sometimes, on their tractors.

I turned my bike around and rode toward home as fast as I could pedal. I had an idea for the next part of my Jimmy Shannon story.

In no time I was home. I pulled in to the yard, slammed on my brakes, spun my bike around, jumped off, put down the kickstand and ran inside.

"Hi, Blake, I didn't expect to see you for a while," said mom looking up from her sewing. "What are you up to?"

"I came home to get my notebook, a pencil, and two oatmeal cookies," I answered. I closed the lid of the cookie jar with cookies in one hand and my notebook and pencil in the other, then headed back out the door.

"I'll be back in a little while," I yelled to mom as I hopped on my bike and rode down the street. I took a shortcut between the sets of gas pumps at **Chet's** Gas Station. In no time I was back at the **Cozy Cupboard**.

"Hi, Mrs. Clark," I said, as I walked into the **"Cozy."** I jumped up on one of the red-topped stools and sat at the counter.

"Hello, Blake, how are you?" asked Clara. "Can I get you something?"

"No, thanks. I'm working on an assignment for Mrs. Elsey, and I'm writing a story about Jimmy. I know he stops here to see you all the time and sometimes he sits on the bench out front," I told her.

"You're absolutely right, Blake. Jimmy often stops here for a snack, before he rides his bike back home," said Mrs. Clark, wiping her hands on her apron.

"Many times when I'm fixing food for people, Jimmy comes in and talks to me while he follows me around the restaurant," she said, smiling as she talked.

"People in town leave money here to pay for Jimmy's food, which is very nice of them," she continued.

"It sure is," I said, writing notes in my notebook.

"Jimmy brings me flowers on special days, and at church on Christmas Eve, he always sings "*Silent Night*" for me. He makes me so happy that it brings tears to my eyes," she said with a wide grin.

"He is such a special person to this town. You can't help but smile when Jimmy's around or even when someone mentions his name," she said.

"I know," I said, nodding my head as I closed my notebook. "Mrs. Clark, thank you for helping me. I have to go now, but I think Jimmy comes here for a Lions Club meeting, doesn't he?" I asked.

"You should talk to your Grandpa about that, Blake," she said. "Your grandpa and Jimmy are both in the Lions Club. They have their meetings here every week. What a couple of characters those two are together!" Mrs. Clark said with a great big laugh.

I put my pencil in my shirt pocket and tucked my notebook inside my shirt.

"Thanks again, Mrs. Clark," I said, as I headed out the door.

"You're welcome, and I'd sure like to read your story when it's finished," she called after me.

"Okay," I said closing the door behind me.

Other Marcellus Stories

Mrs. Elsey was right again. We were busy with our "reporting" and we were having fun. In fact, when we talked to each other and compared stories, all we wanted to do was find out more about Marcellus, its people, places, and things.

"What are you reporters finding out?" Mrs. Elsey asked one morning.

"I found out something about the old train depot," said Terry, looking down at the notes in his notebook. "A long time ago, a man who once ran for president came through Marcellus. The train stopped and he went into the depot, but I can't remember his name," said Terry as the entire class groaned.

"Check your notes again," Doug suggested.

"Wait," Terry said, quickly moving on to another topic, "also a long time ago, there was a train that came through Marcellus and stopped at the depot on its way to Dowagiac. It was called the *Orphan Train*. The *Orphan Train* brought homeless kids from New York City. Some of them got off the train and went to live with families in Dowagiac."

"Very nice job, Terry. We'll look forward to hearing more about what you find out about the *Orphan Train*, **and** the man's name that was running for President," Mrs. Elsey said with a smile.

"Anyone else?" she asked, looking around the room.

Jack who sat at the back of the classroom, raised his hand. Mrs. Elsey pointed at him and nodded.

"I'm researching some people and a thing, Mrs. Elsey," he said. "I've been collecting the names of people from Marcellus who served in the military. Their names are on the big metal plaque that's hooked to the huge rock in front of the library."

"Good idea, Jack," said Mrs. Elsey. "There's important history about the people of our town whose names appear on that plaque."

"How many of you have ever run your hand across that huge plaque that Jack is talking about?" asked Mrs. Elsey. Every person in the classroom raised their hand!

Ann raised her hand extra high, like she was trying to stretch up to the ceiling.

"Yes, Ann, and what have you found out?" asked Mrs. Elsey as she adjusted her glasses.

"Mrs. Schug in the **News** office has been telling me about a blacksmith shop that used to be down by the railroad tracks. She thought maybe there might have been another one in town too. I'm going back to talk with her and find out more," said Ann.

"This doesn't have anything to do with my story," she continued, "but they usually have free candy on the counter in the **News** office."

"That's certainly a good fact to know, Ann," laughed Mrs. Elsey.

The whole time I was listening to my classmates, I was thinking I had to get back to my story. Next on my list was an interview with Mrs. Gooding. I would ride my bike to her house after school.

Getting "Shined Up!"

The wind blew in my face as I rode my bike as fast as I could. I headed west out of town, turned right at the **Wild Patch** Restaurant and rode north on the shoulder of the road. The **Wild Patch** made me think of Jimmy because I had seen him there many times during the summer eating one of his favorite foods … a banana split. My legs were getting tired, as the Goodings' brick house came into view.

I looked both ways for traffic, pulled across the road and rode up the driveway. I parked my bike underneath the basketball hoop at the side of the driveway. I went up the steps to the front porch, taking two steps at a time.

Before I even knocked, Mrs. Gooding was at the front door.

"Hi, Blake," she said. "You're a bit far from home, aren't you? Come on in."

"Thanks," I replied, walking into the living room.

"Let me guess what you're doing here, Blake," said Mrs. Gooding with a smile.

"I'll bet you're here because you're doing a story about, ohhhh, let me guess . . . Jimmy Shannon?" she said.

"How did you know?" I asked.

"A little birdie told me," said Mrs. Gooding with a big smile, "No, really I saw Mrs. Elsey at the grocery store, and she was telling me about your class writing assignment, and how exciting it is."

"Do you want to know about what happens when Jimmy stops here on his way into town?" asked Mrs. Gooding.

"That would be great," I answered, pulling out my notebook and pencil.

"Most of the time Jimmy just stops by to say 'hi' to my husband, my son, my daughter or me," she said.

"But sometimes I have to do some work on Jimmy," she said with a serious look on her face.

"What kind of work?" I asked.

She went on with her story, "About a week ago, I saw Jimmy riding his bike by the house, and I knew there was a dance that night at the church. Of course, Jimmy would be going to the dance, so I yelled out to him and said, 'Hey, Jimba, come on in here and let me 'shine you up.'"

"You **shined** him up?" I asked.

"Well, not exactly, but this is what happened. Jimmy came into the house, and we went into the big bathroom over there. I put a chair right in the middle of the bathroom floor for Jimmy to sit on. Now, keep in mind, I'm not a beautician, but I work on him just because he's my pal," she said.

"So when I shine Jimmy up, he sits right there, takes off his shirt and glasses. I put shaving cream on his face and shave him. I also put toothpaste on the toothbrush, then Jimmy hands me his false teeth and I brush them real well. Next, Jimmy raises his arms into the air and I scrub under them with a washcloth, soap and water. After that, I put on some Old Spice® Deodorant. During the time we're getting him 'shined up', guess what we are also doing?" she asked.

"I don't know, Mrs. Gooding. What?" I asked.

"We laugh, Blake, we just laugh," she said, even laughing right then just thinking about it.

"Then we go out to the kitchen, and that's where I give Jimmy his haircut. After that he's all 'shined up'. Then, Jimmy goes out into the garage through the door right over there," said Mrs. Gooding, looking across the kitchen at the door.

"Why does he go into the garage?" I asked.

"So I can brush the hair off his back. The garage is also where we keep the pop for Jimmy so he can have one when I'm finished 'shining him up'," she said, laughing again.

She pointed to my notebook and asked, "Is that the notebook you're writing your story in? It looks like it's getting pretty full."

"It sure is, Mrs. Gooding. There are so many good stories about Jimmy," I said.

"Jimmy is a pretty special fellow," she said as I bounded down the steps and hopped onto my bike.

"He sure is. Thank you, Mrs. Gooding. I would like to watch you 'shine Jimmy up' sometime," I said with a big wave goodbye.

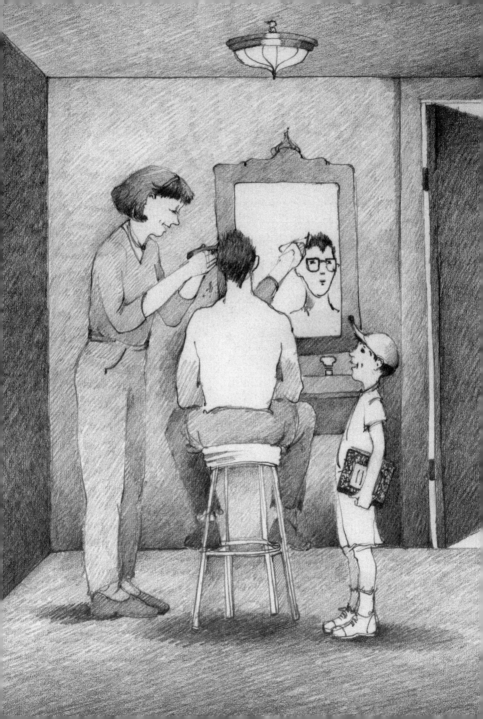

Jimmy Shannon ... SUPERFAN

"Hi Mom, hi Dad," I said, rushing into the house through the kitchen door. "I can't stay long. Right after supper, I have to get over to the gym for the opening game of the basketball season, and I know I'll see Jimmy there."

"Slow down, slow down," said Mom, "We'll get you there with time to spare. Now sit down and eat your supper."

"I'm supposed to meet Grandpa Jack at the game," I said. "I hope he can tell me some sports stories about Jimmy."

After supper, Dad picked up the car keys and asked, "Do you have your notebook and pencil?"

"I hardly go anywhere without it now," I said.

"Let's go!" said Dad. Then we got into the car for the short ride to the high school.

We drove to the entrance of the gymnasium, where Dad stopped the car. Jimmy was sitting outside the gym on the bench that was put there just for him. Many times he had to "wait" before a game, or for school to dismiss so he could see his "pals." As usual, Jimmy was wearing his jacket with the big letters that spelled out **"SUPERFAN"** across the back.

Dad said, "Did you know Jimmy's jacket was purchased by the student council in honor of Jimmy being the best sports fan Marcellus has ever had? He wears that jacket everywhere."

"I'll put that in my story," I said. "I'll see you after the game," Dad said as I pushed the car door shut and ran in the direction of Jimmy.

"Hi, Jimmy," I said.

"Hi," said Jimmy.

"Who do you think will win the game tonight?" I asked, even though I knew what he would say.

"'Cellus win," said Jimmy in his own language that was well known to most everyone in town.

"I'll see you inside the gym," I said as I headed for the front door to meet my Grandpa Jack.

"'kay," said Jimmy.

Grandpa Jack and I walked into the gym. To get the best view of the game we climbed all the way up to the top bleachers. As we sat down, I said to Grandpa, "I've got to do some writing during the game. The next part of the story is about Jimmy and sports, and Grandpa Terrill said you would be the person to help me with this part of the story."

"Your mom and dad told me you were writing a story about Jimmy," said Grandpa Jack, "Of course, I'll be glad to help you because I think Jimmy is one special guy and I think you are pretty special too!" he added with a wink. "Is your pencil nice and sharp?" he asked, "because I can tell you a lot of Jimmy stories."

The gym began to fill up quickly for the big rival game between the "Wildcats" of Marcellus and the "Falcons" of Constantine. I didn't know it at the time, but Jimmy was to receive a special honor at halftime.

"Well, Blake, let me tell you, nobody has seen more games in this town than Jimmy. He attends all the games. You probably know that the team bus picks him up and he rides with the team to all the away games. In football, he leads the team onto the field, and runs so fast the players can hardly keep up with him. During baseball season he sits in the dugout with the team."

"And here's an 'inside' story," said Grandpa, leaning over like the story would be extra special. "I happen to know that one of the players on the team carries Windex® and paper towels in his gym bag to all the games, just so he can clean Jimmy's glasses."

"No way, Grandpa," I replied, thinking he was kidding as he often did.

"Better write that down, it is a true story," he assured me.

"Now back to basketball," said Grandpa.

"Of course you know Jimmy is on the floor with the team and the cheerleaders before the start of every game. He always shakes hands with the team members and coaches. Many times he even shakes hands with the players from the other team before he sits down on the bench with the 'Wildcats'."

Just then Jimmy walked into the gym surrounded by his pals. He had a bag of popcorn and a pop.

"Look Grandpa, there's Jimmy," I said.

"Grandpa, why does Jimmy get to have a pop in the gym when no one else is allowed?" I asked.

"It's a privilege only for him because he is such a loyal fan," Grandpa told me. "Have you ever noticed that Jimmy eats his popcorn one piece at a time?"

"Why's that?" I asked.

"To make it last longer," said grandpa, laughing and nudging me with his elbow.

"And have you noticed Jimmy's picture in the hallway outside the gym? He's in the Marcellus Sports Hall of Fame for being the best sports fan ever," grandpa said.

"I know, Grandpa. I always look at Jimmy's picture when I come to the high school. I hope Jimmy will cheer for me someday," I said.

"I'm sure he will," replied Grandpa.

I had my notebook open, laying on the bleacher in front of me. I wanted to write notes about what Grandpa had just told me.

Just like always, I leaned back against the wall with Grandpa and watched Jimmy out on the floor before the game. He cheered, jumped up and down, greeted the players (from both teams), and shouted "Go 'Cellus," and proved just exactly why he was called the SUPERFAN. Then Jimmy sat down at the end of the bench where the players were all seated.

The basketball game was good, but the halftime was even better.

A microphone was placed at the center of the floor, and the athletic director, Mr. Frye, asked Jimmy to come out to receive an award. Jimmy walked to the center of the floor and stood next to Mr. Frye. He smiled and lightly patted Mr. Frye on the shoulder.

Everyone was silent as Mr. Frye said, "It is with great pride that tonight we recognize Jimmy Shannon for the loyalty, support and friendship he has shown to all the athletic teams and students in Marcellus for so many years. Jimmy, you are truly a SUPERFAN. Through the years the players have often said they wouldn't play as well if you weren't at the games. So, Jimmy, in honor of all you have done and continue to do for everyone, we would like to present you with this SUPERFAN plaque."

Mr. Frye handed the plaque to Jimmy and hugged him. Jimmy had tears streaming down his cheeks as he turned and held the plaque up above his head to show all the people who were now standing in the bleachers on the Marcellus side of the gym. They applauded as Jimmy walked from one end of the bleachers to the other, showing his "fans" the plaque. Jimmy didn't stop when he got to the end of the Marcellus bleachers. He continued to walk across the end of the gym floor until he was in front of the Constantine bleachers. From there he walked with his plaque held high in front of the Constantine fans, who also stood and cheered. There wasn't a dry eye in the gymnasium.

While I was applauding, I looked up at my Grandpa Jack. He had tears in his eyes too.

Say, "Cheese!" It's a Tradition.

Grandpa Jack told me each year when the homecoming dance is held in the gymnasium, Jimmy is invited and has his picture taken with the homecoming queen. Jimmy is always "shined" up and wears a sport coat and a tie. He stands next to the pretty homecoming queen and they both wear a big smile as their picture is taken.

Grandpa said when people in town take pictures of Jimmy, they usually get two copies of each picture. They keep one and give the other one to Jimmy. He has quite a collection of pictures. He has pictures:

- With each year's homecoming queen.
- With his pals.
- Cheering at the games.
- With the teams (boys and girls).
- With individual players (boys and girls).
- Playing in the charity basketball game.
- Winning the "Big Fish" contest.
- On the fire truck in the parade. (Jimmy was the grand marshal at Oktoberfest.)
- With the band.
- On the field.
- On the court.
- With his younger pals.
- Walking into town.
- Riding his bike into town.
- In his Santa Claus hat at the Christmas party.
- Sitting on his bench at the **"Cozy"**.
- Advertising the Lions Club chicken dinner.
- Dressed up for the Lions Club meeting in his sport coat.
- In his Lions Club vest.
- At his birthday celebration.

The "Kitty Cat Club"
Jimmy's Community Service

"Good morning, Mrs. Elsey," I said, as I walked into the classroom.

"Good morning, Blake, how are you this morning and how's your story coming?" she asked.

"Well, I've got a little bit of a problem, I think," I said, with a frown. "My dad told me there's a Lions Club meeting tonight, because it's Wednesday. Since Jimmy is in the club, he told me I should see if I could go to the meeting to get more information for my story. I don't know if I can go because I'm not a member of the Lions Club. I'm not sure what to do."

"I might be able to help you," said Mrs. Elsey. "Mr. Porath is the president of the Lions Club."

"Do you know him, Mrs. Elsey?" I asked, wondering how that might help me get into the meeting.

"Yes I do, Blake. In fact, when he was in fifth grade, he sat right over there in the same row you're in," she said, pointing toward a desk.

"You had Mr. Porath in school?" I asked with surprise.

"Yes I did. In fact, I had lots of the club members in class."

"Wow, Mrs. Elsey, that's cool!" I exclaimed.

"I'll tell you what, Blake," she continued. "You go on down to the meeting tonight at the **Cozy Cupboard**. I'll make some phone calls before you get there, and I'll just bet they'll let you in. You know they are pretty nice people," she said.

"Okay, Mrs. Elsey, thank you very much," I said, heading toward my desk.

"You're welcome, and let me know how the meeting goes," she said, as she walked into the classroom behind me.

Wednesday Evening at the "Cozy"

I peeked through the big front window at the **Cozy**. The only people inside were Mrs. Clark and Jimmy. Mrs. Clark was in the back of the restaurant preparing food. I could smell the fried chicken.

Jimmy was busy setting the tables. He had already set up the Lions Club flag and all the smaller flags at the front table. I sat down on the bench outside the front door and hoped I could get in for the meeting and some of Mrs. Clark's fried chicken.

I was looking through my notebook when the club members started arriving shortly before six o'clock.

Mr. Porath pulled up in his blue pickup truck and parked in front of the **Cozy**.

As soon as he got out of his truck, he waved and said, "I thought you might be here tonight, Blake. Sounds like you have a pretty big assignment you're working on. I remember those big assignments when I was in Mrs. Elsey's class."

"We're glad to have you here, so come on in," Mr. Porath said as he held the door open for me.

Jimmy and Mrs. Clark both looked up from their work and smiled.

"Mr. Porath, what does the Lions Club do?" I asked.

"We keep the lions out of Marcellus, and keep the town safe," he said.

"We don't have any lions in Marcellus," I replied with a chuckle.

"That's because we're doing such a good job," said Mr. Porath as he laughed and tapped the top of my head.

"I'm just kidding you," he went on. "We're what you call a service club, which simply means we help people, not only here in town but around the world. We are known for helping people to see better by providing glasses to those who need them, but cannot afford them. The Lions Club also provides health screenings, builds parks, supports eye hospitals, gives scholarships to young people to help with education expenses, and when there is a disaster somewhere, the Lions Clubs help in any way they can."

"One of the things the Lions did right here in our own town was to provide an eye test for Jimmy and then pay for his glasses."

Mr. Porath patted Jimmy on the back and said, "Hey Jimmy, who got those nice glasses for you?"

Jimmy smiled and said, "Kitty Cat Club."

The Meeting

The time passed quickly, and it wasn't long before all the club members were there, seated and ready to start the meeting. Mr. Porath called the meeting to order. It reminded me of the way Mrs. Elsey started the school day. The first thing Mr. Porath did was introduce me as their "special" guest.

I sat next to him at the front table. He explained to me what was happening during the meeting.

The meeting started with everyone standing up, saying the Lions Club pledge and then singing the first verse of the song *America*.

I watched Jimmy through most of the meeting. He sat patiently and looked around at everyone.

"Blake, any time we discuss an idea or a project we think the club should become involved with, we have to vote to see if a majority of the club members think it's a good idea," Mr. Porath explained.

"We do that at school sometimes," I replied.

Mr. Porath continued, "First, someone has to make a motion, then someone has to second the motion, so we can vote on the idea."

"The someone who seconds the motions is Jimmy. He seconds **all** of our motions. We just have to look at him, and he knows to say 'second.' It's just one of his jobs. Jimmy is a very important member of our club. He carries a sign up and down Main Street to advertise our chicken barbecue during the summer. Before every meeting, he comes several hours early to help Mrs. Clark get everything ready.

Jimmy **never** misses a meeting."

I thought the meeting was interesting but the best part was after the meeting, when we got to eat. Clara Clark is a very good cook. When everyone had their plates filled and began to eat the delicious food, the room got very quiet.

Then someone said to Jimmy, "Where were you at the last meeting? We sure missed you."

Jimmy just laughed. He knew they were "kidding" him again. Jimmy was wearing his yellow Lions Club vest. It was covered with award pins for all the things he had done for the club. One of the pins was for perfect attendance. Jimmy hadn't missed a meeting in ten years!

There was one more time Jimmy was "kidded" before the night was over. When Mrs. Clark served everyone a big piece of her delicious homemade apple pie for dessert, my Grandpa Jack said, "Somebody stole my pie! Was that you, Jimmy?" He looked at Jimmy and pretended to be serious.

Jimmy just laughed because he knew Grandpa Jack had made the pie "disappear" by holding his plate out of sight under the table.

After dessert, it was time to go home. Mrs. Clark stood by the door saying goodnight to everyone. As Jimmy was leaving, she handed him a bag with several pieces of pie inside. "This is for a snack later," she said with a wink. Jimmy gave her a big smile and a big hug.

More Jimmy Stories

My notebook was getting full of Jimmy stories. I had heard so many stories, I couldn't write them all down. Everyone had a favorite Jimmy story. In one story, Jimmy was one of the best teachers in town, even though he had never been to school. In another story Ron Welburn, owner of the **Wild Patch** Restaurant, had to have heart surgery. While he was in the hospital, flowers were planted around the restaurant in no particular design. No one knew how they got there.

It seems that *someone* wanted Ron to be okay, and thought if *he* planted flowers, it would help. It must have helped, because Ron recovered. That *someone* often visits Ron and Patsy at the restaurant on his way home, and usually has a big banana split.

In yet another story, people in town talked about Jimmy's loyalty. When his mother was sick, Jimmy rode his bike eight miles to the nursing home and back to visit her every single day for three years. **Jimmy never missed a day**. When the weather was too bad to ride, he walked. Sometimes a friend would give him a ride. Nothing seems to stop Jimmy, he just keeps moving forward. Jimmy's fuel is love, loyalty, and friendship.

On the Bus

Mrs. Lofts was standing next to the open door of her school bus as the kids bounced down the two steps and jumped to the ground before heading into the old school building. From kindergarten through high school, this is where everyone went to school. It was the only school in town.

Their bus driver, Red (nicknamed for her bright red hair) knew all her riders and wished them each a good day as they passed by her each morning. Red was also the bus driver for the high school basketball team. And of course, she knew Jimmy because he rode on the team bus to every game.

"Hi, Mrs. Lofts," I said, walking on the sidewalk in front of the bus on my way into the school.

"Good morning, Blake," she replied. "How's 'the story' coming along?"

By this time, it seemed everyone in town knew about my story.

"How did you know about my story?" I asked.

"Jimmy is one of my favorite passengers," she said.

"Say, have you written about the time Jimmy was given an honorary diploma at the high school graduation?" she asked.

"No, I haven't. It's on my list, but I'm not sure who to interview about that," I replied.

"I think you should talk to Miss Cobb. She was a teacher in the high school, and has been the scorekeeper at the basketball games for over fifty years," said Mrs. Lofts, nodding her head. "She'll record the points that you make when you get into high school someday, Blake. Miss Cobb is what you call a 'fixture' at the basketball games."

"What does a 'fixture' mean?" I asked.

"It means that she's always there, behind the scorer's table, seated not very far from Jimmy, who's always sitting on the bench. You can count on it, Blake, they'll both be there." Red continued.

"Miss Cobb knows Jimmy very well and she was at the high school on the day Jimmy got his diploma. I think you should talk to her. I would like to read your story when it's finished," said Red, as she turned to get back on her bus.

"Okay, and thanks," I replied.

I wondered how I was going to get my story to everyone who had asked to read it. Oh well, I would think about that later.

I headed into school just as I heard the first bell ring.

Recalling a BIG Day

I was on my bike . . . again.
I had my notebook tucked into the front of my shirt . . . again.
My pencil was in my pocket . . . again.
I was on my way to do another interview . . . again.
And I was excited . . . again.

It was Saturday morning, and I was headed to Miss Cobb's house.

I rode my bike down the street past the library, across Main Street, past the **Pork Chop's Diner**, over the railroad tracks, and two blocks to Worden Street. I made a left turn and headed east on Worden Street. I rode three blocks to the end of the street, and arrived at Miss Cobb's house.

I parked my bike and walked up to the door on the front-screened porch. Miss Cobb was waiting for me with a smile.

"Good morning, Blake, come on in," she said, holding the door open. "Have a seat."

I walked over and sat down in the big wicker chair near the corner of the porch and took out my notebook and pencil.

"So you're writing about Jimmy," said Miss Cobb, "By the looks of your notebook, you've already got a few stories."

"You wouldn't believe how many stories there are about Jimmy," I said.

"And since Jimmy is a special guy, I'll bet there are some very nice ones," said Miss Cobb.

"That's for sure, and I'm hoping you'll tell me the story of the day Jimmy got his diploma," I said, as I opened my notebook.

"It was quite a day, Blake, not only for Jimmy but for everyone in town," she said. "It was a beautiful, sunny Sunday afternoon. The whole town was headed to the gymnasium for graduation. It was a celebration, and everyone was all dressed up and happy. There were moms, dads, brothers, sisters, aunts, uncles, grandmas, grandpas, nieces, nephews, cousins, teachers, and friends of the seniors who were graduating. Everyone was also excited that Jimmy Shannon would receive his honorary diploma that day."

I was writing quickly in my notebook. "What happened next, Miss Cobb?"

"Well, when everyone was seated in the gym, the band began to play a graduation song. All the seniors began to march into the gym in single file, with a space of about six feet between each person. They were all wearing their caps and gowns."

"Were the caps those funny looking flat things with that stuff hanging down on the side?" I asked.

"Yes, and that 'stuff' hanging down is called a tassel," she said with a grin.

"When Jimmy walked in through the gym door, kind of "shuffling" like he sometimes walks, you know—you've seen him, Blake, holding his hands together in front of him with a smile on his face. Everyone in the gym stood and applauded for Jimmy," said Miss Cobb.

"Jimmy just looked around as he walked, at all of his friends, his 'pals,' the 'kids,' all standing and applauding. He had tears rolling down his cheeks as he walked with the rest of the seniors. The seniors helped him find where he was to sit for the graduation ceremony. I looked around, Blake, and most of the people there were wiping tears from their eyes. Everyone was so happy," said Miss Cobb.

"I think it's strange that sometimes we cry when we're happy!" I said.

Miss Cobb nodded and continued, "Everyone settled back in their seats. The graduation speaker was introduced and walked over to the podium to give his talk. The speaker had grown up in Marcellus and had been one of my students. He is now an author, storyteller and sculptor. He knows Jimmy Shannon very well and is very fond of him.

"And guess what the speaker talked about?" asked Miss Cobb.

"I give up, what?" I answered.

"He talked about Jimmy and our town, and what they mean to each other and how we are all connected," said Miss Cobb.

"Then the seniors went up on stage one by one as their names were called. They walked across the stage and shook hands with Mr. Jensen, the superintendent. He handed them their diploma with his left hand and shook hands with each of them with his right. Then they walked back to their seats and sat down."

"When Jimmy received his diploma, he first hugged Mr. Jensen, then he went over and hugged the speaker, who also had tears in his eyes.

Then Jimmy walked over and hugged all the members of the band because they were his pals too."

"I'll always remember the next part of the story. Jimmy held his diploma up over his head with both hands so everyone could see it. Everyone applauded as he walked back to his seat," said Miss Cobb.

"I've got one more thing to show you, Blake. Hang on just a second," she said, as she got up and walked from the porch into the house.

When she returned she had a plate of Windmill cookies, a glass of milk and an old copy of the **Marcellus News**. She handed me the cookies and milk, and then opened the newspaper.

"Look at this, right here on the front page," she said, pointing to a picture. "I saved this paper to remember that special day."

There on the front page of the newspaper was a close up picture of Jimmy wearing a cap and gown. He was holding up his honorary diploma with a huge smile on his face.

"What a great picture of Jimmy," I said. "Thanks for the story, the cookies and the milk. I really like these cookies."

"You're welcome," said Miss Cobb, "and of course being a teacher, I'd really like to see your story when you get it finished."

"Thank you Miss Cobb, seems like everybody is telling me that," I replied.

In no time, I had my notebook tucked in my shirt, my pencil in my pocket, and was back on my bike headed toward home.

Great News

Monday morning at school, with everyone seated at their desks, Mrs. Elsey printed in large straight letters on the chalkboard: **GREAT NEWS**.

Everyone was curious. We could hardly wait to hear the great news.

Mrs. Elsey smiled as she told us: "Over the weekend, I had the good fortune of having lunch at the **Cozy Cupboard** with Mr. and Mrs. Moormann and Mrs. Schug. During our conversation, we talked about your 'investigative' writing projects. Not only were they interested in your stories, but they said they had heard other people around town talking about the assignment."

"Now class, it is very nice just to know people are interested in what we're doing, but there's even more," she said.

"Together, they came up with an idea that is quite exciting. They would like to put all of your stories in a special section of this week's **Marcellus News**. Then everyone in town will be able to read what you have written, just like real reporters' stories."

"So we need to get down to business," said Mrs. Elsey, "if we want to finish up and meet our deadline for the paper."

Terry raised his hand and asked, "When's the deadline?"

"I need to deliver all of your stories to the **News** office by Tuesday at five o'clock," she said.

"That's tomorrow," I said.

The Final Interview

After school, once again I was on my bike with my now well-worn notebook and pencil, headed to Jimmy's. I had to write the final part of the story which was about Jimmy's house.

When I rode up in front of Jimmy's house, Jimmy was on the front porch doing something you usually don't see him doing. He was just SITTING!

"Hi Jimmy," I called and waved.

"Hey," said Jimmy waving back. "What you doing?" asked Jimmy.

"I'm writing my final story about you, Jimmy. It's about your house—and, guess what, all of the stories about **you** and Marcellus are going to be in the newspaper this week," I told him, trying to get the words out as fast as I could.

As soon as I mentioned the house, Jimmy was up heading toward the front door. He turned around and motioned for me to come inside.

Jimmy's house is near a small lake which is perfect, because Jimmy loves to fish. The people of Marcellus built the house for him. It is one-story, very neat and tidy and has a wooden deck on the front.

Inside the house, no matter where I looked, there was something that told about Jimmy, his pals, and "his" little town. There were pictures, notes, newspaper articles and plaques on the wall telling of his accomplishments, dedication and loyalty.

Jimmy proudly showed me around his home. He showed me the hot dogs in the refrigerator and the pudding cups in the cupboard. Besides banana splits, these were two of Jimmy's favorite things to eat. There was also a big piece of chocolate cake wrapped in Saran Wrap® sitting on the counter. I knew someone had given that to him for a snack.

"How do you cook a hot dog?" I asked him.

Jimmy pointed to the small microwave on the counter.

"How do you know when the hot dog is done?" I asked

"It 'splodes'", he said with a giggle.

I quickly wrote 'splodes' in my notebook on the page labeled, "Jimmy's vocabulary".

"Do you like living here, Jimmy?" I asked.

He smiled and nodded his head up and down several times.

I knew that some of Jimmy's friends stopped by each day to see if he needed anything and to make sure he was okay. Teresa lives nearby. She and Jimmy are great friends. Jimmy helps her with chores and she helps Jimmy with things around his house.

While I was writing in my notebook, Jimmy went to the refrigerator, reached in and took out two bottles of pop. He handed one to me.

"Pop," Jimmy said.

"Thanks, Jimmy," I replied.

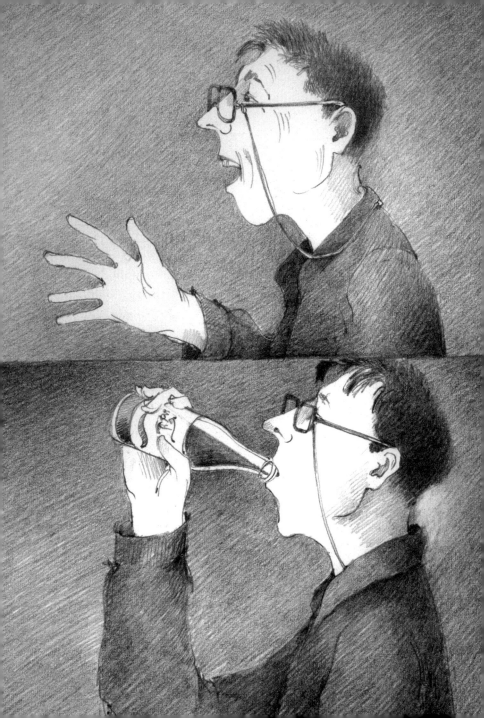

Jimmy watched quietly as I had finished my writing and my pop. I said, "Thanks, Jimmy. I have to get home to finish my story so I can turn it in to Mrs. Elsey tomorrow."

"I'll get you a copy of the paper," I told him. "I'll read it to you, if you want me to."

"'Kay," said Jimmy.

Jimmy patted me on the shoulder and waved as I got on my bike and left his house.

On my ride back into town, I thought about my story and how my problem was solved as far as all the people who wanted to read it. All our stories would be in the special section of the paper, and everyone in town reads the **Marcellus News**.

The closer I got to town the faster I pedaled. I wanted to get home to finish my story about Jimmy Shannon.

The Final Chapter

On Wednesday morning when Mrs. Elsey walked to the front of the class to start the day, everyone wanted to know what had happened after she turned in the stories.

"Well, class, this has been a week of good news, hasn't it?" she asked. "When I dropped your work off at the **News** office yesterday after school, Mr. Romig was there. He told me he will bring a special bundle of papers to our room just as soon as they're printed. You'll each get two free copies of the paper."

We all cheered and Mrs. Elsey smiled.

"I went through each of your stories before I turned them in at the **News** office," she continued. "You should be proud of your great work and the fact that you completed your stories on time. I've lived here all my life, and I still learned many new things from your stories. They were wonderful to read. I thank all of you for doing such a great job."

Then, Mrs. Elsey had each person in the class come to her desk one at a time so she could talk to them briefly about their papers . . . and even though it wasn't Friday, she gave each of us a piece of her delicious peanut butter fudge.

When I went up to her desk, Mrs. Elsey said, "Blake, your story about Jimmy helped to show how much he is *included*, *accepted*, and *expected* to be a part of our community."

"Thanks, and thank you for the fudge too," I said. "Can I ask you something, Mrs. Elsey?"

"Of course," she said.

"What would happen if people outside our small town read the stories about Jimmy Shannon?"

Mrs. Elsey paused for a moment, looked at me, then said with her special smile, "Well, Blake, I think they just might learn something or perhaps they will remember something about life that they might have forgotten."

Jimmy's Vocabulary
(Understood by everyone in his Small Town)

$1 – "Big one"

$5 – "Big big one"

$10 – "Big, big, big one"

$20 – "Really big one"

Any red produce - (strawberries, tomatoes, etc.) "The red ones"

Anything related to wood – "The stick"

Anything mechanical (bike, car, etc.) – "The thing"

Baseball team – "The birds" (because they eat sunflower seeds)

Fishing, one of his favorite things to do – "Chishing"

Frank Townsend – "Hank"

How he knows when a hot dog is done in his microwave –
  "They Splode!"

Jerry Townsend – "The monkey"

His friends in town – "Pals"

Junior varsity team – "The little ones"

Kalamazoo – "The big town"

Lion's Club – "The Kitty Cat Club"

Leon Kindt – "Him"

Marcellus – "Cellus"

Santa Claus – "The red man"

Students at the schools – "The kids"

Sue Kindt – "Her"

The Kindt farm – "Kent and them"

Varsity team – "The big ones"

When asked what he wants to eat – "I'm not picky"